MOON GIRL AND DEVIL DINOSAUR

This Is Moon Girl

Written by **Tonya Leslie, Ph.D.**

Illustrated by **Gianfranco Florio**

MARVEL

Los Angeles • New York

This is Moon Girl.
She is a Super Hero.
Her super-power is her super brain.

Moon Girl can solve any problem.
All she has to do is think.

Moon Girl makes special gadgets
in her lab.
She made a Bubble Blaster!
She made rocket booster skates.
She uses them to fight crime.

Moon Girl has a sidekick. . . .

Devil Dinosaur!

Moon Girl brought Devil Dinosaur
through a portal.
It was an accident.

Devil Dinosaur is a loyal friend.
He helps protect the neighborhood.
He loves Moon Girl more than anything.

Well, almost anything.

Moon Girl keeps
her neighborhood safe.

She makes Moon Girl magic!

Moon Girl is Lunella Lafayette.
She is thirteen years old.
She lives in New York
and goes to middle school.

Lunella loves to roller-skate
through her neighborhood.
It's called the Lower East Side
(or the LES).

Whoosh!

When Lunella skates she feels free.

Everyone in the neighborhood
knows Lunella!

Lunella's family owns a business.
It's a skating rink called Roll With It.
Her whole family works there.

Pops runs the rink.

Mimi is in charge of the snack bar.

Dad helps with the business.

Mom is the DJ.

Lunella's family works together.
They live together, too!

It can get a little noisy.
But there's always a lot of love.

Lunella has her own bedroom.
She spends a lot of time there.
That's because it holds
a big secret.

There is an elevator in her closet.
It goes to a special place. . . .

Moon Girl's secret lab!

Lunella's best friend is
Casey Calderon.

Casey helps Lunella.
She helps Moon Girl
and Devil Dinosaur, too.

Casey is a great partner
for Moon Girl.

She is also a great friend
to Lunella.

Having a secret is hard.
But someone has to
keep the neighborhood safe.

It's a big job.
That's why it takes a Super Hero
with a super-sized brain.

And a sidekick named Devil
Dinosaur!